Tales for TINY TOTS

CONTENTS

SANDLE BROTHERS LTD, LONDON W.14
A PENTOS COMPANY

The Naughty Little Hare

There was once a little blue bear called Bruno who often played in his woodland home with his friend Scamper, a young hare. The two friends would have great fun together, racing from tree to tree, playing hide and seek, and jumping the stream—although Bruno often fell in with a splash when they played this game! Still, the two friends would laugh until tears ran down their cheeks and the sun had dried Bruno's wet fur, and then they'd start all over again.

But sometimes Scamper was very naughty and teased Bruno, and one day when the little bear asked the hare to play with him, Scamper replied rudely, "Oh, no,

I don't play with ugly blue bears! Today I shall go and
pick some flowers and play in the wood with my friends
the butterflies and the little rabbits. Goodbye!"

Poor little Bruno began to cry, and Trill, a little bird
who was sitting on the branch of a nearby tree, called
out: "You are a naughty hare, Scamper, to be so unkind

to Bruno! And it is not very wise to go deep into the wood, because there are many dangers there. You had better stay here where it is safe and play with your little friend."

But Scamper only shrugged his shoulders carelessly, and with four big leaps bounded off into the woods.

Little Bruno sobbed harder than ever, and Trill called after the hare, "It will serve you right if you come to some harm, you naughty little Scamper!"

But Scamper did not hear the little bird's angry words. He was already deep in the heart of the wood, busily picking pretty flowers, surrounded by hundreds of lovely butterflies.

Suddenly a small rabbit came running by, and as he passed he shouted to the little hare: "Reynard the fox is heading this way, Scamper, looking for a tasty morsel for his dinner. Hurry up and run away as fast as you can!"

But Scamper was rooted to the spot with fear as he cried despairingly: "Oh, Trill was right, it is dangerous here! How I wish I had stayed to play with

Bruno!"

At that moment up ran the fox and seized Scamper quickly. "Aha, this is my lucky day," the fox chuckled. "This tender young hare, cooked with onions, will make a lovely meal."

Reynard tied Scamper securely to a tree while he

10

started to collect some wood to make a fire.

As Scamper watched him in fright, great tears rolled down the little hare's cheeks, and he longed to be safely back playing with Bruno.

"Bruno, Bruno, where are you?" he cried sadly. "If you would only come and rescue me from this nasty old fox I would never be unkind to you again!"

But the little bear was too far away to hear Scamper's urgent pleas. Bruno was listening to Trill and his bird family telling him lovely stories, for Trill was trying to help the little bear forget all about Scamper's unkindness to him. And it worked too, Bruno was entranced by Trill's stories. Especially the one about the bluebird who would fly high up into the sky, way above the clouds, right up to the tips of the sun's rays, just to say: "Good morning, Sun."

Suddenly, just as Trill was about to begin another story, a tiny rabbit burst into the clearing and called to a tiny group: "Please come quickly, my friends! Reynard the fox has caught

your friend Scamper and is going to eat him. If you don't come at once it will be too late!"

Trill and Bruno immediately forgot all about Scamper's rudeness and unkindness to them, and they begged the little rabbit to show them the place where Scamper was being held prisoner by the fox.

They hurried through the woodland until the rabbit motioned them to slow down and keep quiet.

"There they are," he whispered, pointing to a clearing near a big oak tree.

Bruno gasped with horror as he saw Scamper tied to the tree while the fox was busy lighting a fire beneath a large black pot, ready to put the little hare in it.

Bruno was suddenly very angry, and seizing a heavy branch he rushed out from behind the tree where he was hiding, and hit the fox with his stick.

"Don't you dare eat my best friend!" he shouted, and he chased the fox all the way back to his den, hitting him hard with the tree branch all the time, while Trill and his family pecked Reynard's bushy tail with their beaks.

As the fox fled down into his den, Bruno called out after him: "If I ever find you in this part of the wood again, chasing Scamper or any other of my friends, you will be in very serious trouble . . . so take care!"

"Oh, I promise never to harm anyone

again!" called the fox quickly, for he was afraid that the brave little bear might follow him into his den and start beating him again.

"Good! Now let's go back and free Scamper!" cried Bruno to his bird friends.

So off they hurried, and while Bruno put out the flames

of the fire, Trill and his family quickly untied the ropes that bound Scamper.

"Oh, thank you all for coming to my rescue!" cried Scamper, leaping about happily. "I didn't really deserve it because I was so rude and unkind to you, but I promise that from now on we will all be the best of friends, and Bruno shall be my very best friend of all!"

The little hare kissed Trill and all the other little birds, and he gave Bruno a really big hug . . . and he even politely thanked the little rabbit who had come to tell his friends about his capture by the fox. Scamper didn't forget anyone, he really had turned over a new leaf.

So, if you are ever passing through a certain leafy wood and you see a little bear and a little hare busily collecting pretty flowers, you can be certain that it is Bruno, the little blue bear, and his friend Scamper . . . the little hare who isn't naughty any more!

THE BRIGHT RED BALL

Spring had returned to Sunshine Valley. Leaves covered the trees, and the meadows were green once again, while violets and timid little daisies peeped out shyly from mossy banks in the woodland.

All the woodland animals who had slept away the cold winter months now awoke to welcome the spring. Among them were two little squirrels called Skip and Sprite, who came out of their nest a little sleepily, but who were very glad to see that spring had returned at last.

They found their store of nuts and berries, which they had hidden away before they had gone to sleep, and after a lovely breakfast they ran down the tree and across

the grass to play.

Suddenly, right in front of them, the little squirrels saw a bright, red ball. It was something they had always dreamed of finding one day.

Skip and Sprite began to toss it to each other happily, but then suddenly it bounced over the branches of the

18

trees and into the long grass right in front of the house of Mr. Prickle the hedgehog.

Skip and Sprite were very glad to discover that the hedgehog had gone out for a walk, for they were afraid that he might have burst their magnificent ball with his prickly spines . . . and then all their lovely games would be over!

Then, suddenly, Skip and Sprite heard a small voice saying: "Little squirrels, may I play with you?"

Skip and Sprite looked around in surprise and there, behind a tree trunk they spied what looked like a little bundle of yellow feathers with a red beak and two red feet.

"Who are you?" asked the two squirrels together.

"My name is Downy Duckling," the little creature replied, "and I would so much like to play with you."

But Skip and Sprite laughed so loudly when they heard this that Downy was frightened and fell backwards on the grass.

"How can *you* play with us!" mocked

Skip. "You're too small, and you can't run quickly like us. Stop getting under our feet. Go away, so that we can get on with our game."

Sprite nodded in agreement and so, sadly, the little duckling walked away. But he hid behind a clump of bushes and watched the two squirrels throwing the ball

to each other.

Then, suddenly, Skip tossed the ball too far, and it fell with a plop into a tiny lake nearby.

Skip and Sprite gazed at each other in dismay as the ball floated about on the lake, for being squirrels neither of them could swim.

Then Sprite had a good idea. "Listen, Skip, I will hold onto the branch with my paw, and you stick tightly to my other paw and see if you can stretch out and reach our ball."

Skip did as his brother suggested but, unfortunately, the branch that Sprite was holding was too light to bear all the weight . . . and the two acrobats were hurtled down into the water!

Fortunately they landed in a shallow part of the lake, and although thoroughly drenched the squirrels were able to struggle back safely to the lakeside, where they sank sadly down upon the grass, and wondered what to do next.

Then Skip cried suddenly: "Why don't we go and ask the old owl what we should do? He knows everything, he does, and

he's sure to know the best way to get our ball back!"

So, as quickly as they could, the two little squirrels rushed over to the owl's house, where they saw him perched on the top of a gigantic pine tree.

He was just dropping off to sleep, but as soon as he saw the squirrels, he said in his harsh voice: "I saw it all, so

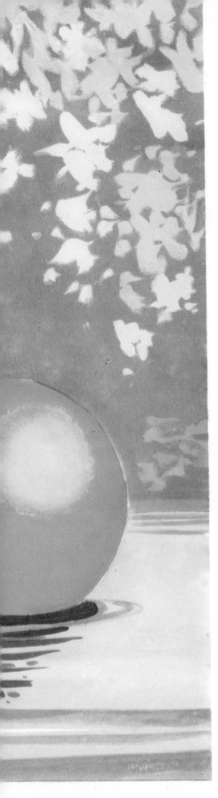

there's no need to explain. There's only one person who can help you to get your ball back, and that's the little duckling you chased away. . . ."

The owl had not finished speaking before Skip and Sprite hurried away to find Downy.

There he was, still waiting patiently behind the bushes, sad and lonely.

"Is it true that you know how to swim?" asked Skip eagerly. "A little," replied Downy, shyly.

"Please will you get our ball from the lake?" begged Sprite. "If you do, we will let you play with us."

"Certainly," replied Downy, and in a trice he had plunged into the water and was pushing the red ball towards the bank with his beak.

"Oh, thank you, Downy!" cried the squirrels in delight. "Come along and play ball with us."

So the three little friends played happily together until evening, and Skip and Sprite found a deserted fox's den to hide their precious ball away until morning.

The squirrels were just about to say goodnight to Downy and settle down to sleep, when suddenly the little duckling spoke.

"I've just thought of another amusing game we can play," he said. "Follow me down to the lake."

Their curiosity aroused, the two little squirrels did as

they were bid, and Downy pointed to a tree trunk lying on the bank.

"Help me to push it into the water, and we will all go for a sail," he chuckled.

Skip and Sprite climbed carefully onto the trunk as it floated gently in the lake. Although they felt a little afraid, they were rather excited too.

Downy put a piece of red ribbon around his neck, and Skip held the other end of the ribbon, and the little tree boat floated gently across the lake, with Downy leading the way, and cleverly guiding the boat.

The three little friends laughed as they sailed along and sang a little song:

Let's toss the ball,
Toss! Toss!
Let's sail on the water,
Sail! Sail!
We're having such fun
With our friend the duckling,
Hurray, hurray, for Downy Duckling!

And the moon up in the sky looked down and laughed too.

The Adventures of the Little Yellow Duckling

One summer evening, Goldie, the little yellow duckling, tied a large handerchief containing a few grains of corn to a long pole and crept quietly out of the house.

Shouldering his burden bravely, Goldie looked up at the starry sky and said firmly: "Now I am off to China."

Goldie was the smallest duckling in the family, and he had the brightest yellow feathers of all his brothers and sisters.

Because his feathers were so yellow his mother sometimes teased him by saying, "You are a funny little yellow duckling, to be sure. Why, you look like a little Chinese duckling."

When Goldie asked about the Chinese, Mother Duck told him that these people had yellow skins like his feathers, and that they lived in a faraway land called China.

Goldie was very pleased to hear that there were actually men who looked like himself, and he decided that one day

he would go and visit them.

Tonight was the start of his long journey.

Goldie crossed the big meadow where he lived with his family, and he slipped out of the farm gate.

Soon he came to a pond on which swam a duckling as yellow as himself.

"Are you Chinese?" called Goldie loudly. But the duckling never answered him. "Perhaps the Chinese can't speak," said Goldie, as he went on his way.

Goldie crossed over a bridge which led into a dark wood, but through the leaves of the trees he could see a big yellow ball in the sky.

It seemed a very long way away to the little duckling, and so, raising his voice, he called out loudly: "Are you Chinese up there?"

"No, that's only the moon," chuckled a voice beside him.

Turning round in surprise, Goldie saw a large animal standing beside him. The creature was so big that poor Goldie trembled with fear.

"Are you a Chinese person?" he

stammered timidly.

"Oh, goodness gracious, no!" laughed the stranger. "I'm Growler, the blue mountain bear. But what is a little duckling like you doing out in the wood so late at night? It's time you were tucked up safely in bed. You might get a nasty fright if you stay here . . . wicked animals prowl

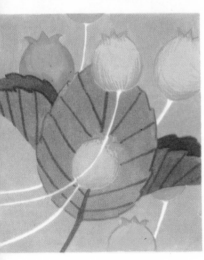

around here at night."

Realising that the bear was friendly and meant him no harm, Goldie began to boast a little.

"I'm off to China," he said. "Do you know where it is?" When Growler looked amazed and shook his head, Goldie added with a mocking smile, "Fancy you not knowing that, a big bear like you! I'll call and tell you all about it on my way back."

And, with a cheery wave, Goldie left the mountain bear and went on his way, while Growler stared after the little duckling and looked very worried.

Goldie walked through the wood for what seemed like miles and miles. Suddenly, in the far distance, he saw two shining yellow lights.

"Hurray, I must have arrived at last!" he cried joyfully. "Those are yellow lights, so they must be from Chinese houses."

But as he drew nearer poor Goldie got a dreadful shock. They weren't house lights at all . . . they were the two great round eyes and the open mouth of a

terrible hungry beast.

Goldie tried to run away, but a giant paw stretched out and held him fast.

"At last, a tasty bit of duckling for my dinner!" growled the beast. "I am Wolfgang, the wicked wolf of the wood. Nobody ever passes by my lair without

ending up on a plate for my dinner."

Poor Goldie sobbed at these words, but suddenly he was thrown onto the grass. The wolf had been forced to release him because he himself was being attacked by the blue mountain bear.

Kind Growler had been afraid that some harm might come to the foolish little duckling and so he had followed Goldie. Now he had come to Goldie's rescue, and he chased away the wicked wolf while the little duckling watched with gratitude.

As he lay on the ground near an old oak tree, all Goldie's desire to go to China disappeared. He was cold and tired, and all he wanted to do was to go home to his mother.

"Oh, Mother, where are you? Please come and look for me!" Goldie cried, as two tears rolled down his face.

"I will look after you until morning, little duckling," said a gentle voice at his side. "And tomorrow I will take you home again."

"Who are you?" stammered Goldie.

"Don't be afraid, I am Mother Hind,

and I have children of my own," said the gentle creature, as she made Goldie comfortable with the pillow and coverlet she had brought with her. "Sleep now, little duckling, and I will stay near to watch over you and keep you from harm."

She bent down to kiss Goldie gently on his beak, but

the little duckling was already asleep and dreaming sweetly.

Next morning, Goldie thanked Growler for rescuing him from the wicked wolf, and then he climbed upon Mother Hind's back and together they sped away, through the wood.

Soon they reached the farm again, and Goldie received a very warm welcome from his mother and all his brothers and sisters.

"How glad I am to be home again!" he cried, as Mother Duck hugged him. "But I have had some exciting adventures. Listen and I will tell you all about them!"

THE KITTEN WITHOUT A NAME

One day in the attic of a little cottage in the country three little kittens were born.

"You are the most beautiful kittens in the whole world!" cried their mother, as she gazed proudly at them. "And you shall all have pretty names."

The first kitten had soft, soft fur as black as soot—there wasn't a patch of white anywhere. In fact, he was almost invisible in the dark corner where they lay. "I'll call you Blackie," his mother said, "because you're as black as the night sky." Now, Blackie's brother was the complete opposite, his fur was soft, just as soft as Blackie's but it was white. "As white as snow," his mother

murmured when she looked at him. "I'll call you Snowie."

But looking at the third kitten—who was neither black, white, grey or even brown—she added gently, "I will wait until you grow up a little before giving you a name, my little one."

Soon the kittens were strong enough to play about in

the yard, and although Snowie and Blackie were very well-behaved their little sister was always getting into mischief.

She chased the hens, fell in the pig food, teased the cows and chased the birds, if there was any mischief to be found, this little kitten was always in the middle of it. Hardly a day went by without something happening, and that usually meant that she got very dirty in the process, her mother got very tired of having to wash her all the time. Especially as the little kitten disliked being washed anyway. "I don't think that daughter of mine will ever grow up into a nice young lady," her mother cried more than once.

When her friends learnt that she had no name, they suggested to her that she was called Mischief, because she was always up to tricks.

But the little kitten wanted a prettier name than that and, learning one day of a wonderful dog named Perry Palette who spent all his time among his paint pots, painting anything or anybody who

came his way, the little kitten resolved to go and see him to ask him if he could help her.

So, without a word to anyone, the kitten went off to see Perry, and told him all about herself.

When she had finished, Perry laughed and said kindly: "Soon your troubles will be over. I will paint on you a

lovely blue dress, so that everyone will envy and admire you."

But, unfortunately, as the blue paint touched the kitten's fur it changed to a bright shade of green.

"Oh dear, this will never do!" murmured Perry to himself, and he hurriedly added some smart black stripes over the green, hoping to improve the kitten's appearance.

Finally Perry tied a lovely bow of red ribbon around the kitten's neck and sent her back to her friends.

But, sad to say, none of the kitten's family or friends recognised her when she arrived home. In fact, they were all rather frightened of this green-striped stranger and they ran away from her.

But this did not worry the little kitten, who was rather proud of her new appearance, and she decided to show off a little.

The farmer's wife had put out a line of washing to dry, and the naughty little kitten decided to pretend to be a tightrope walker in a circus, and walk along the clothes line.

All went well for a few moments and then, suddenly, her paws slipped and the mischievous little kitten fell into a large tub of soapy water on the ground below.

The poor little kitten was very frightened indeed, and she called out for someone to save her.

But her mother and brothers were busy looking for mice

in the barn, and although her other friends returned when they heard her cries none of them could swim, and so they were unable to help the little kitten.

As the little kitten struggled to get out of the soapy wash tub, her friends sang a little song:

Oh, how she struggles
To get out of the water,
In her coat of black and green,
The soap makes her fur
Shine and sparkle,
She's the cleanest cat we've seen.

At last, sneezing and blowing soap bubbles, the little kitten managed to struggle out of the tub. The soapy water had washed off all the paint, and the kitten was her original colour once again.

Feeling very sad and sorry for herself the little kitten shook her fur dry, and then climbed back onto the line. She crept into a sock which was drying there, and snuggled down, hoping nobody would see her and start laughing again at her misfortunes.

At last, tired and weary after all her

adventures, the little kitten fell fast asleep in the sock. She was still asleep when the big yellow moon peeped at her from behind the clouds.

But when she woke up next morning the sun was just rising, and its bright rays touched the little kitten's fur, making it shine like gold.

The little kitten yawned sleepily, and then jumped out of the sock and walked cleverly along the line, just at the moment when a little girl arrived at the farm for some milk.

"Oh what a beautiful little kitten!" she cried. "I will ask if I may have her for my very own. Would you like that, little kitten?"

The little kitten purred loudly and rubbed her back against Susan's leg.

"My name is Susan," said the little girl, bending down to stroke the little kitten gently. "And when you come to live with me I shall call you Honey . . . because that is just the colour of your beautiful gleaming coat."

And so, at last, the little kitten was given a pretty name of her own.

The SPARROW in the STRAW HAT

One day Mother and Father Sparrow were waiting rather impatiently for the last of their eggs to hatch out.

They already had quite a large family, all of whom had arrived on time, but this last little sparrow was very late in being born.

At last Father Sparrow said to his wife, "We cannot wait for him any longer, my dear. We must make the lazy little fellow come out of his shell!"

So, together, the two elder sparrows began to peck the shell with their beaks, so that the top began to break open.

Suddenly, out of the open shell popped a cheeky little

sparrow wearing a straw hat ... his parents were surprised!

"Well, you certainly are the cheekiest little sparrow I have ever seen!" chuckled his father. "And the first one to pop out of a shell wearing a hat. We will call him Cheeky, eh, my dear?"

His wife nodded, and soon all the family were welcom-

ing their new brother, and calling his name from the treetops.

"*Cheep . . . cheep . . .* Cheeky's come at last!"

The days passed and soon it was time for Cheeky to go to school for the first time. The schoolmaster was an old blackbird who taught all the young birds to build a nest, hunt for food, and defend themselves against their enemies in the woods.

So, of course, school was very important, but naughty Cheeky always found some excuse not to go.

Usually he disappeared just before school started, and did not arrive back until it was over . . . and one day he didn't arrive home at all, which worried Mother and Father Sparrow very much.

That day, Cheeky had gone, with some other mischievous sparrows who loved to play truant from school, to a wood by the side of a mountain where they knew they could get some mulberries.

The sparrows ate and ate, and Cheeky was so greedy that when he had finished

he fell fast asleep. When he woke up all his friends had flown home because it was night time.

Cheeky tried to find his way home, but he was hopelessly lost, so he found a tree near a stream and went to sleep again.

Next morning he flew down to the stream to bathe and

have a drink. Immediately he was surrounded by several blue and red fishes who asked him all about himself.

"I'm Cheeky, the sparrow with the straw hat, and I come and go as I please, so mind your own business," replied Cheeky rudely.

Then he slipped into the water and got soaked and all the fishes roared with laughter.

Cheeky flew off again, but when he saw two huge butterflies, the lazy little bird persuaded them to carry him on a swing made from thread which the butterflies kindly carried between them.

Cheeky loved being carried through the air on his swing, and he would not have minded if the butterflies had flown about all day. They flew high above the fields and then swooped down to brush the bright flower petals with their wings. Cheeky was having a lovely time. "This is much better than boring old school," he said.

But, suddenly, down on the ground below them, Flutter and Flitter, the two butterflies, saw a strange menacing

51

figure in the field. It was only a scarecrow put there
by the farmer to stop the birds from stealing his corn,
but it so frightened the two little butterflies that they
dropped the thread they were holding and flew off quickly.
Cheeky then lost his swing, and he tumbled down
through the air and landed with a bump, right at the feet

of the frightening old gentleman.

Turnip Top, the scarecrow, was quite a friendly old soul, but poor little Cheeky did not even wait for him to speak.

His little heart thumping with fright Cheeky ran off through the cornfield, scared to look back in case the ragged stranger was following him.

He ran through the bumpy fields, weaving in and out of the waving golden corn, and right into a dark forest. It was very quiet and the trees were very tall. They waved their long spiky, knobbly branches at him sternly as if to say: "You shouldn't be here, you know!" Cheeky felt very small and very frightened.

At last, worn out by his travels, he fell asleep, and poor Cheeky slept, not for a few days or even weeks . . . the little sparrow slept right through the autumn into winter.

In fact, the day he awoke the first snow was falling and, as lost as ever, poor Cheeky set off through the snow to try to find his way home.

It was a long, slow journey, made

even more difficult by the falling snow. Poor Cheeky found it very difficult to find anything to eat, as the ground was frozen and hard and there were no berries on the trees.

On and on the little sparrow travelled, until at last, with tears running down his cheeks, he sat down in the snow.

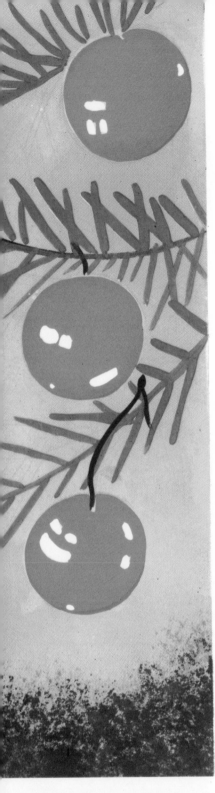

"All is lost, I can go no further! Oh, how I wish I had been a good little sparrow and gone to school. If I had, I would now be snug and warm and happy at home!"

Suddenly through the snow came Mother and Father Sparrow. They had never given up hope of finding Cheeky one day, and each day they had searched for him.

"Look, my dear, a little sparrow in a straw hat with a red ribbon around it!" cried Father Sparrow.

"It's Cheeky, come home at last!" cried his mother joyfully, as she ran to greet her little son.

Cheeky's mother and father helped him home to their warm nest, where his brothers and sisters welcomed him happily.

"Happy Christmas, Cheeky!" they chorused. "We *are* glad to see you!"

And they gave him lots of .delicious red cherries to eat . . . Cheeky's favourite treat.

The tales of TINKER and TINY

One bright morning, quite by chance, a little dog named Tinker was walking through a wood when he met a little mouse.

"Hello," said the mouse cheerily. "My name is Tiny and I am off to seek my fortune so that I can help my large family back home in Spain."

"Why, what a coincidence!" cried the little dog in surprise. "I, too, am seeking my fortune. I have come all the way from Switzerland, where I have left my six dear little puppies."

"Suppose we join forces and seek our fortunes together?" suggested Tiny. "Two heads are better than one, and perhaps we will get rich all the quicker."

"Agreed!" cried Tinker, shaking the little mouse warmly by the hand. "Now what shall we do?"

"Have you any ideas?" asked Tiny shyly.

"Let me think a minute," replied the dog. "*Hmm*, can you sing?"

"A little," admitted Tiny. "Why do you ask?"

"Then we will earn our living as entertainers!" said Tinker eagerly. "I have a fine voice, so people should pay us well."

"I hope so," murmured Tiny, as he and his new friend strode off to the nearby town.

"Of course they will," replied Tinker, as they stood

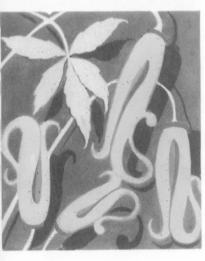

beneath a lighted window and started to sing.

But alas for Tinker's fine hopes! They had scarcely sung more than a few bars when a bucket of cold water was thrown over the two singers and an angry voice called out: "Stop making that horrible noise and be off with you or you'll get another bucket of water!"

"Come along, Tiny, this is no place for us," shouted Tinker, and the two friends rushed away.

The next place the singers tried was a fine restaurant. Tiny jumped onto a table, ready to sing a sweet serenade.

But before he could start, a lady called out: "Look, a mouse, a mouse, get rid of it, someone!"

And poor Tiny had to flee for his life, while Tinker also decided not to sing there either.

"Nobody seems to appreciate our singing," said Tiny sadly, as he climbed on Tinker's back that night on a bench in the park. "We have not earned a penny yet."

"Never mind, there's always tomor-

row," comforted Tinker. "Snuggle down now, my little friend, and go to sleep. Goodnight."

"Goodnight, and sweet dreams," murmured Tiny.

And a moment later the two friends were fast asleep, dreaming of the families they had left behind them.

Next morning the two friends were awakened by a

merry voice calling to them: "Wake up, my friends, it is a lovely day. My name is Monty. Who are you, and what are you doing here?"

Opening their eyes, Tinker and Tiny saw a cheeky little mouse smiling up at them.

Tinker quickly told the little mouse all about themselves, and how they planned to make their fortune.

As he finished speaking, Tinker jumped down from the bench, and Tiny and Monty stared at him in astonishment. Then they both burst out laughing.

"The bench on which you slept last night must have been newly-painted," chuckled Monty. "The paint was still wet and now you are covered with stripes . . . you look just like a real Bengal tiger!"

Tinker looked down at himself in dismay, but suddenly their new little friend laughed.

"That gives me an idea. Why don't the three of us become a circus act? I know exactly what to do, because I used

to live in a circus tent."

The others thought this a splendid idea, and the three of them worked hard at perfecting a clever acrobatic act. Tinker was a tiger with Tiny in a splendid turban on his back, and Monty was the clever animal tamer.

At last they were good enough to perform in a real